Natural Law

TINA RIFFEY

Publishing Coordinator – Sharon Kizziah-Holmes

Paperback-Press
an imprint of A & S Publishing
Paperback Press, LLC.

ISBN -13: 978-1-960499-29-5

DEDICATION

To those who have a fickle muse that won't let you get onto another story until you finish the one she/he just dropped, but won't help you with it either.

Authors Note

This is the result of three drabbles that my muse dropped off one night. I think she wanted it to be a prequel to a series. At least that's what it turned out to be. However, the series will have to wait as I have several others higher in the queue to do.

If you would like to check out my other books
you can visit my new website at
https://tlriffey.wordpress.com.

And if you like this novella please rate/review. Authors love the feedback and readers find it helpful.

PROLOGUE

You'd think cops would be used to the weirdness that happened around Halloween. People went crazy during that time, more so after the vampires, shifters, and immortals came out of hiding.

You'd be half right.

We expect the weirdness, but not the quantity or quality of it. And the Special Circumstances Division of the police department got a lot more business during this time of the year. The Others it seemed were not immune to the craziness just because they were not 'humans'. SCD took care of all crimes that involved vampires, shifters, or immortals. However, 'humans' were still top of the heap when it came to violent crimes. That didn't mean the Others weren't violent but there were still more humans being the perp.

My partner's phone rang, and he answered it with

"Dufort."

I stopped typing my report and looked over at him when he hung up moments later with a scowl. "Louis?"

"That was Doyle."

We had met the wolf shifter on a murder case two weeks ago. I had had to reveal my secret during that case because the perp had been an elemental like me. Elementals were generally despised by the Others and were boogie men to humans. Humans don't like anything that science can't make them understand.

"What did he want?"

"Our help." Louis stood and checked his weapon at his belt. "He said your talents may be needed."

I stood and checked my weapon in its shoulder holster. Though if this concerned my kind the gun would be useless, but my knife was handy as always. "Did he give you any details?"

"No, just the address. The warehouse district by the old docks."

That was the old part of the city.

We hurried out of the bullpen and got on the back elevator. The front lobby would be crowded so we would go out the back. Besides, we parked in the back when we came in after lunch an hour ago. We had planned to do paperwork this afternoon, but it looked like that plan was shot to hell. The back elevator dropped us off at the back corridor and we rushed down the hall and out the door.

I slid into the driver's seat before Louis could. As long as I was able I would drive. Louis' driving was terrible. We'd be there faster, that is if we made it there at all. Louis grumbled as he got into the passenger side, but I ignored him and was soon heading into traffic.

It took us a little over twenty minutes to get to the warehouse district. I rolled down the window and took a deep breath. Next to freshly turned dirt, the smell of the water here was my favorite scent. "Which warehouse?"

Louis pointed ahead and to the left where a hatchback and an SUV were parked, and I pulled in alongside.

The two large wooden doors were shut, but the smaller human sized door was open, and a familiar short figure was standing in the doorway.

Now I'm used to feeling like a mousy nerd next to Louis' All-American good looks, but Doyle's dark ruggedly handsome good looks just made me feel very self-conscious. Not that I didn't think I look alright but they both made me look so plain Jane that I was developing a complex. I really wish vampires and shifters had ugly mugs, but plain looks didn't get them prey or sympathy. Sorry, volunteers, I mean. Gotta be P.C.

Louis and I got out of the car and headed to the door. Once there Doyle didn't say anything just led us deeper into the building. We dodged stacks of crates and miscellaneous debris until we came to a small open area.

Two bodies with severed heads lay strewn there. Two feet away from them was an open grill leading under the floor.

I carefully knelt by one of the heads and gently tilted it to look at the face. It was one of the vampires we had met on the same murder case we had met Doyle.

Vampires didn't turn to dust when you beheaded them like Hollywood made you think. However, they did dry up and become mummies after a while depending on their age. The younger they were the longer they were corpses and the older the quicker they became mummies.

"I've been keeping an eye on them," Doyle said. "Since that case. Late this morning they tore off to this place. When three hours passed and they didn't come out, I entered and found this."

"There's a maze of tunnels under these warehouses," Louis said.

"If he went down there," I said as I stood. The warehouse was a maze itself and one could easily hide in it.

"He did." Doyle seemed confident.

"Who wants to go first?" I asked.

Doyle immediately jumped down.

I followed, landing in a puddle of water.

The tunnel stretched on both ways into the semi-darkness. Small bare red bulbs dotted the stone ceiling, and a stream of water covered the unseen floor. The walls were coated with concrete which was chipped here and there. It wasn't a sewer tunnel for which I was grateful.

Louis landed beside me and immediately began to bitch about his now-ruined shoes.

I jabbed an elbow into his ribs, and he shut up.

"With all this dampness I can't get a scent," Doyle told us.

"Callista?"

I knew what Louis was asking. Reaching out to the elemental plane, the Aether, I squatted and touched the water. “Revelare.”

Glowing boot prints appeared in the water stretching out in front of us.

Both men stared at the boot prints, surprised.

I didn't normally do things like this as it would get me killed, but since no one else was around I made an exception. Usually I just touched the Aether and asked for a direction, then it would draw me towards who or what I wanted.

Withdrawing my hand from the water, I stood, and the boot prints became barely visible. After all I wasn't really touching the water except through my shoes. “Shall we?” I asked, gesturing to the faded boot prints.

Doyle immediately set off with me behind him and Louis bringing up the rear. We followed them for what seemed like hours, though my watch reassured me it was only forty-five minutes, until we came to a tiered junction. The water we had been walking through ended at the first tier, pooling and running to the sides where small drains were. There were three entrances. One entrance went straight ahead, the two others branched off right and left.

We stopped before the first tier and stared at the entrances, the water running over our shoes now.

Doyle's nose flared, but then he shook his head. “Still too much dampness.”

“I'm taking that tunnel.” I pointed to the tunnel that went straight. There was no tug so one tunnel was as good as another. I waded through the small pool, then stepped up onto the first tier. “If you find him, text me.”

Louis pulled out his phone. “No service.”

“Mine neither,” Doyle said after he pulled his out and looked at it.

“These tunnels lead somewhere. And that somewhere will have service,” I told them. I knew they were reluctant to split up, but it made sense.

They returned their phones to their belts and went up past me to the second tier where the other two tunnels branched off.

The bare bulbs continued on in my tunnel, so I stepped into it without hesitation. There was a slight bend to it so I couldn't see very far, but enough to see the tunnel was empty ahead. I kept my eyes moving as I walked along, looking for any other tunnels or drains leading off, but the walls seemed solid. What these tunnels had been used for in the past I didn't know but they were empty and unused now.

I came upon an archway and stopped. At one time it had been bricked up, but not now. Several bricks had been removed from the center to make a large human size hole. It was dark on the other side.

At the warehouse there hadn't been a hint that the perp was an elemental, and he was for sure not a water nymph or the boot prints wouldn't have shown. So I drew my gun and pulled out the small flashlight on my keychain. The keys went back in my pocket, and I flipped on the flashlight. It wasn't much but better than nothing. Now how to enter in case the perp was waiting by the entrance.

I squatted and leaned in, leading with my

weapon and flashlight.

What I could see looked like a basement. Cement brick walls and pipes. There was debris everywhere and crates. It was very dim, barely light enough for me to see more than a few feet in front of my face without the flashlight. I saw no one but I heard a noise like a compressor running.

I straightened into a crouch and moved into the room. With the flashlight on I was an easy target, so I flipped it off and clipped it to one of my jeans' loops. The compressor noise would make it hard for me to hear anything until I was right on it and the same for the darkness.

Feeling my way along, I moved cautiously deeper into the basement. A bunch of crates loomed on my right.

Suddenly the crates fell toward me, one hitting me hard and making me fall to the floor. A boot stomped on my wrist, and I let go of the gun involuntarily. My wrist was suddenly free, and I heard the gun go skittering across the floor as I rolled away. I sprung to my feet into a fighting stance, but I couldn't see my assailant in the darkness. The noise of the compressor still interfered with my hearing.

Before I could do anything something barreled into me, knocking me down to the floor again, this time on my back. The perp then knelt on me, making it hard for me to breathe.

I flicked my wrist, then drove my small knife into his eye. His dead weight fell on me, and I immediately shoved him off. I lay there a moment just breathing, then got to my feet. Rolling him onto his stomach, I then reached for my zip ties in my back pocket. I didn't trust that he didn't have a cuff key somewhere on him.

He would stay comatose until I pulled the knife from his eye. I had felt his immortal aura when he had knelt on me. But even if I hadn't known he was an immortal I still would have stabbed him. He had meant to kill me. I got that loud and clear.

After I was sure he was secure, I unclipped my flashlight from the jean loop and switched it on to get a better look at the perp.

His long blond hair was in a ponytail, and he was wearing jeans and a Tee. What I could see of his face was ordinary looking, less so with the knife sticking out of his eye, but nobody I'd think twice about walking down the street. Well, the sword at his belt would have given me pause. Though a lot of immortals still carried them they weren't as fancy as this one. The sheath and hilt were made of silver with what looked like diamonds and rubies. It looked more like a ceremonial sword than a real one.

I pulled out my phone and hit the GPS feature. According to it I was still in the warehouse district. I sent my location and a brief text to Louis before returning my phone to my belt. Using the flashlight, I searched for my gun and spotted it near a bit of debris. As I retrieved it, I got an uneasy feeling.

Suddenly a light was shone in my eyes. I froze.

Noises to my left told me there were more than one person—vampires my gift said. It sounded like they were picking up the perp and dragging him away.

"I'd like my knife back," I told them. Something skittered across the floor and bumped into my boot. Hopefully it was my knife. It would be hard to replace it as the blade had been custom-made.

The light just as suddenly shut off.

I blinked several times to try and clear the after image. But of course they were gone by the time I could see anything. I shone my light down and there was my blade by my boot. At least they had been polite enough to return it, though shinning the light in my eyes had not been polite at all. I returned the knife to its place before flashing the light around.

Only the fallen crates, the small pool of blood, and the disturbed dust on the floor showed that anything had taken place here.

"Callista?!"

That was my partner's voice.

"I'm here!" I yelled back.

A light bobbed into view, then my partner joined me.

"Where's Doyle?" I asked him

"Following the vampires that have the perp. We showed up just as they shoved the body in their car, so he went after them when they sped away."

I didn't know what Doyle was after, but I did know why the vampires wanted the perp. "You know Riley's case, the one about the vampire beheadings?"

"Yeah. Someone broke into several vampires' places and beheaded them. The word 'Rache' was written somewhere near the bodies so Riley suspects revenge as a motive. What has..." He paused. "The perp is the killer?"

“Yep. Got a reading off him when we fought.”

“Well, well, well.”

“Another tidbit—he's immortal.”

Louis took in a sharp breath, then let it out in a flat whistle.

As a rule, immortals didn't go insane or let their desires dominate them, unlike vampires. They usually had a reason for how they acted, especially concerning violence. Of course, there were the rare cases, but the impressions I got from the perp didn't point to insanity.

His phone beeped and Louis checked it, then stuck it back on his belt. “We need to get back to the station. Lab results are back on the Robertson case.”

I glanced around one more time, then followed him away. There was nothing more for us to do here and there was a murder to solve.

Chapter 1

A Week Later

You'd think after running yourself ragged over a child kidnapping The Powers That Be would give you a break when you solved it satisfactorily.

You'd be wrong.

Well, maybe TPTB would, but a Lycan wouldn't. At least Doyle didn't.

My partner Louis and I were detectives in the Special Circumstances Division of the Lansdell Police Department. SCD got all the cases that involved shifters, vampires, and immortals. A human child had been kidnapped by a grieving shifter who had lost her own child. It had been an impulsive crime of opportunity. But the shifter's pack had run interference and she had been good at avoiding us, so it took three days of almost non-stop hunting to catch her.

I had been down for about two hours when my phone woke me up. I wasn't in time to answer it, but it beeped with a text message. The message just had an address and the word 'hurry' so I dragged on the clothes I had just stripped off and hurried out the door. I sent a message to Louis before I left the parking lot of my apartment.

Louis was leaning against his parked motorcycle when I arrived at the address. He looked rested and for a second I envied his vampire biology. But only for a second. There are too many negatives factors that come along with the positives.

I got out of the car and we both approached the door.

It was an old tenement building next to an abandoned lot and didn't look lived in itself. However the lock and buzzer on the battered door were new.

I pressed the buzzer, and a pinpoint of red light touched my chest for a moment. Looking up in the corner where the door met the cover, I saw a small camera. The door buzzed and Louis and I entered. I made sure the door was closed behind us, then followed the short hallway to the lobby/foyer area.

The room had been turned into a large lounge area with couches, chairs, pillows, and a large TV. This building was a Den for a pack. However, the lounge was empty except for Doyle who was standing by a half-concealed door at the back of the room.

“Why are we here?” I asked him as soon as I saw

him.

"Come with me," he said, opening the door and stepping inside.

I looked at Louis who shrugged, then moved to follow Doyle, my partner at my heels.

We went down a short hall, passing a few closed doors, to the stairway at the end. The stairs ended at a basement landing with a steel door and concrete walls. A security camera was mounted in the ceiling and above the door.

This must be the pack's safe room.

Doyle unlocked the two deadbolts and opened the door an inch. "It's me, Kiran," he said. "With the two I told you about."

There was rustling, then, "Come on in."

The Lycan opened the door wide and motioned us in.

In front of us was a gigantic room set up like the lounge above. To the left was a kitchenette with an attached office while to the right was an enormous platform bed. But I only gave everything a glance before turning my full attention to the man and woman on the platform bed. The man was holding the woman who was wrapped in a sheet and looked to be unconscious. Her red hair had been chopped off crooked at her neck and what I could see of her body was covered with welts and bruises.

It took me a second, but I recognized the man as the immortal killer from last week. However, what really shocked me was that my gift told me the woman was an elemental.

"Explain!" I snapped at Doyle.

But it was the immortal that spoke. "Two months

ago, vampire enforcers broke into our home and took Skye. I killed a few of them before they managed to get away with her. There were just too many and Skye's not a fighter. Well, she is but..."

"I know what you meant," I told him and gestured for him to continue.

"I've been searching for her ever since. Then I got a lead a few weeks ago that lead me here to Lansdell."

"We had been hearing more rumors," Doyle said. "In the last few years concerning vampires going rogue, breaking Charter. Which wasn't surprising to us, but two months ago the rumors got strange, and the local vampire council became even more insular. We knew something was up. I volunteered to investigate."

"We as in the city's shifter council or as in the local Lycan packs?" I asked. Doyle had been careful not to say which, but this was too important for side-stepping and misunderstandings.

"The packs," he said reluctantly. "The shifter council dismissed our concern as our strong hatred of the Vampire."

"That's why you were following the enforcers," Louis said. "To see what the vampire council was up to."

"Yes."

"Vampires kill elementals." Everyone knew this. They may have to be sneaky about it because of humans but it happened none the less.

"They want a home-grown one of their own," Doyle said.

I blinked. A docile elemental in vampire hands.

That wasn't even worth thinking about. Just no. I looked at Doyle and raised an eyebrow. He nodded and I frowned. “There's little chance that her child would be an elemental.”

It was Doyle's turn to raise an eyebrow.

“No genetics involved.”

Doyle just stared at me.

This incomprehension was why we were feared. Our gift couldn't be explained by science. It had to do with the spirit, the soul which meant faith, not proven facts and that wandered into religion territory. Something that humans—and the Others—had strong feelings and ideas about.

I made a dismissive gesture, then looked at the immortal. “May I approach?”

The immortal—Kiran, I remembered Doyle called him, studied me for a moment, then nodded before looking back down at the woman.

Keeping my movements easy, I walked to the bed and squatted. The woman—Skye, the immortal had called her, was unconscious. I touched her forehead and reached out to the Aether, searching for her.

Lightening lashed across where her connection was. It was raw. Something had damaged and almost severed her connection. Had she been conscious she would have been in a lot of pain.

I deadened the connection and sent a jolt of energy to awaken her before leaving the Aether. Withdrawing my touch from her forehead, I leaned back on my heels and waited.

Seconds later, her eyes opened and latched onto mine. Fear flared in their deeps.

“You are safe,” I told her. It was true enough for now.

“Skye,” Kiran whispered, and her eyes flashed to his.

I stood, then moved away, letting them have their moment. “You obviously busted them out of wherever the vampires were holding them,” I said to Doyle. “Did you get away clean?”

“No.” He shook his head before moving to the desk in the kitchen where two monitors set. A red light was flashing on one. “I had hoped we could move them before the enforcers caught up.”

“I gather we have visitors?”

“Just two so far. Probably scouts. We have several places around the city, and they wouldn't know which we went to.”

“They know someone's here with the car and motorcycle outside.”

“But neither is the van we escaped in.”

Louis spoke up then. “I hope you hid it well away from here.”

“I had a pup take it to Carson Street and leave it unlocked.”

“Good idea. It's chopped up by now,” Louis said with a grim smile. Carson Street was better known as car jack alley. Vehicles were stolen from the parking lots there on a regular basis.

“Sister,” the woman, Skye, called.

I turned and looked at her.

She was still laying with her head in Kiran's lap but was curled on her side now facing me. I could see the deep weariness in her, yet her eyes still held a spark.

“I'm not a Healer,” I told her. “My talents don't lie that way. I only numbed you so you would have a clear mind.” I paused. With my next words I was risking more than two lives--and breaking a promise. “You have a choice before you. I can cut your connection to the Aether but as raw as it is you'll have bad headaches for the rest of your life. If you wish to keep your connection, you will need Healing because it is killing you right now.”

“Skye,” Kiran's voice was rough with emotion. “Please.”

She patted his leg but kept her eyes on me. “Your mentor is a Healer,” she stated. “You're risking her safety for me.”

“Not for you, the baby.” My first element is after all Earth, the nurturer, the Mother. My instincts always get me into trouble, one way or another. Earth after all did have a dark side as well as a few have witnessed. But the nurturing Mother was in control right now.

She stared at me for a minute, then looked up at Kiran before her eyes returned to me. “I wouldn't ask for this sacrifice...”

“Skye...”

Her fingers touched his lips and he subsided. “But for the child I would. It is the innocent in this.”

“Then we must move quickly. The numbness only lasts for a short time.” I looked toward Doyle. “Are our guests still out there?”

“I don't see them, but that only means they're out of camera range,” Doyle said after another look at the monitors. “But they didn't enter the building.”

I turned to Louis and raised an eyebrow.

My partner frowned, then looked at the monitors himself before nodding. “I'm game,” he told me as he drew his weapon and checked it, then walked to the door. “These should only be scouts but if we wait others might show.”

Kiran helped Skye sit up, then he got to his feet before assisting her off the bed. He steadied her when she swayed, pulling her against him.

I drew and checked my own weapon while they got up, then looked at Doyle. “You coming with us as rear guard or staying here?”

Doyle smiled, which was more a baring of teeth than a grin.

CHAPTER 2

I'd prefer sneaking out a back door, but my car was out front. Louis and I were standing by the front door with Kiran and Skye just behind us and Doyle as rear guard. The last look at the monitors hadn't shown us the vampires and looking out the small window in the door didn't reveal them either.

"You'd best change," I told Doyle. "Unless you want to be at a disadvantage."

Doyle immediately dropped to the floor, convulsing. The skin of his cheeks seemed to tear open to reveal black fur that dripped clear fluid as his face elongated into a snout. His clothes ripped as fur covered muscles burst them apart at the seams and his body changed shape. Seconds later amidst the ruin of his clothes stood a large slick black wolf. He was easily the size of a Great Dane.

I unlocked the door and quietly opened it, my

eyes darting around the shadowed parking lot. It was late afternoon, nearly evening, and the building's shadow lay in front of us.

Louis slipped out and stationed himself a few feet in front of the door.

When nothing happened, I motioned to Kiran and Skye and stepped out with them close behind me. Still nothing happened so the three of us moved toward the car. Once we were half-way to the vehicle though the two vampires came around the building. I pushed Kiran and Skye toward my car while Louis moved to intercept the two vampires. As I opened the back door I heard Doyle snarling and the sound of fighting, so I shoved the other two in the back of my car and hurried to get in the front myself. Backing out, I glanced over and saw two more vampires coming around the building. Flooring it, I got us the hell out of there. Louis and Doyle could take care of themselves, and Kiran and Skye were my responsibility right now.

I slowed down once we were clearly away. We didn't need any attention right now.

"You sure this healer of yours won't mind us just showing up?" Kiran asked as Skye settled curled up on the seat with her head on his lap. I knew the numbness would be starting to wear off.

"She probably already knows we're coming," I told him as I headed toward the outskirts of the city. "Nothing surprises her."

Kiran grunted, then turned his attention back to Skye, running the fingers of his one hand through her hair as he stoked her head.

I took several short cuts, so it wasn't long until

we hit the outskirts of the city. Here it was more rural and less businesses. At the correct driveway, I turned in and drove back through the bit of trees that separated it from everything around it.

At the end of the drive there was a house with two outbuildings. The house was a typical two-story farmhouse and looked to be in need of TLC. I pulled up in front of the house and parked.

Cora came hurrying down the stairs and rushed over to the car. To look at her you would not think she was one of the most powerful Elementals there was. She looked like someone's elderly grandmother, white-hair in a bun, shawl, and all.

I got out of the car and gave her a hug. I wasn't a hugger, but she just made you do it. “Cora.”

She returned the hug, then stepped back and gave me a once over. “That vamp seems to be taking good care of you.”

Though they had never met, Cora knew all about Louis and my job. How I didn't know. She just seemed to know things. If it was part of our gift, she'd never shown me how to do it. Skye moaned and I got back to business. “Cora, this is Kiran and Skye. They need help.”

Cora opened the back door and leaned in, laying a hand on Skye's forehead, making Skye sigh in relief. “Let's get her inside before the others arrive. They're not far behind you.”

“What?”

“Check your car. I wouldn't doubt they put a tracker on it.”

Cora and Kiran helped Skye into the house, and I began to search my car for a bug. Wasn't long before I found it either. It was stuck to the back bumper. I dropped it to the ground and crushed it, though the damage was already done.

Walter came around the corner of the house and trotted toward me. I met him at the steps and greeted the old wolf shifter with a pet and a smile. This place was actually his.

A black SUV with tinted windows came out of the trees and parked behind my car. Four vampires in black suits exited it and moved to stand a few yards in front of us where we stood at the foot of the front steps.

Touching the Aether, I could sense others nearby, but I kept most of my attention on the four in front of us. They were my responsibility. “You're trespassing.”

The one vampire glanced at the badge and gun clipped to my belt, then raised his eyes to my face while the others kept their eyes on either Walter or the front door behind us. “As soon as we retrieve what belongs to us, we'll go.”

“There's nothing here that belongs to you,” I told him.

“That's where we differ,” he said.

“Slaves are forbidden by the Charter.”

“She's a Blood-Bond mate.”

“I highly doubt that.”

“Doesn't matter what you think,” he growled. “I claim her one and as such you will give her to me.”

“Not likely.”

“Then I will take her.” He made a gesture, then frowned as he glanced at the woods to the right and left. Continuing to frown he made the gesture again but still nothing came out of the woods.

Walter made an impatient noise.

"I agree," I told him before looking at the talkative vampire. "Had you taken time to look you would have seen that this is Pack land."

The vampires all looked at Walter who was grinning wolfishly at them.

"But you should be more worried about me."

"You're a police officer," the vampire dismissed.

"I'm a Justice of the Peace."

All the vampires looked at me.

I knew they had heard that phrase before in their legends. The Others all had legends about the ones that enforced the original Peace between the vampires, shifters, and immortals. Ones rumored to be the Elementals themselves. It was all just rumors because nothing was written of that time. Oral tales passed down through the ages. But believed none the less as truth.

The vampires fanged up, their nails turning to claws and their eyes glaring red. They rarely went this far as this would disconcert humans and could cause an incident that couldn't be covered up. But they weren't worried about that right now, I knew. They were right to be afraid of what was going to happen.

Because of their nature the Others were more aligned with the Earth element than humans were. Humans were a balance of Earth and Water, but the Others were Earth with just a touch of Water. Too bad for the vamps that while my main element is Earth my secondary is Water.

I reached out through the Aether to the vampires

as they sprang toward me.

Dust and drops of water sprayed me as I sat hard on the steps behind me. Only a few Elementals could do what I just did, and it wasn't a certainty that we could do it every time. Stripping a being down to their elements was as dangerous to the Elemental as to the subject. I could have been dissolved as well. But I really didn't have much of a choice.

A hand touched my shoulder and I felt soothing waves of healing energy spread into my body. I sighed, then made a protesting noise. Skye needed her more right now.

"Hush, child," came Cora's voice from behind me. "I sent her to sleep, and the Pack will take care of the vehicles so all you have to do is rest."

"Too bad you can't do that to the other bodies," came Walter's baritone.

"Walter." Cora's voice was chiding.

I heard him grunt, then walk away.

The soothing waves of energy slowed, then stopped and Cora's hand dropped from my shoulder. I was still weak, but I was no longer dangerously drained. Opening my eyes, I glanced up at the darkening sky, then looked over my shoulder at Cora. Even though she didn't appear tired I knew she had used a lot of energy to revive me and would be using a lot more to heal Skye. But she never seemed to exhaust her inner well. I wish the same could be said of me.

She straightened, then helped me to stand, keeping a hand on me as I swayed. "As much as I'd like to chat with you," she told me when I steadied.

"You need to get back to the inner city."

"A warning?" I asked.

"I just know you need to get back quickly."

I glanced toward the front door.

"Don't worry about them, they're my responsibility now. Just get going."

I gave her a sloppy salute and headed to my car.

One of the Pack members trotted from around the corner and got into the SUV. He backed the vehicle out then drove it down the drive toward the main road as I got into my own car.

I backed out and then headed toward the main road myself. Skye and Kiran would be well taken care of and kept out of the vampires' hands. Cora would see them along the underground railroad for Elementals, named after the original as it did the same thing, move them to safety. I could go back to my life and not worry about them.

Once back on the main road I took short cuts to get back to my neighborhood quicker. I stopped at the local drive-thru before continuing on to my place.

As I pulled into my parking spot, three vehicles pulled into the lot. One was a squad car, the second was a department sedan, and the third was a SUV. They surrounded me.

I got out with my food and leaned against my car door as the others unloaded. My captain got out of the sedan while two vampires left the SUV. This was not good.

"Where were you, Detective?" my captain demanded.

I held up the fast-food bag. "I woke up and was

hungry."

The two vampires from the SUV snorted and one of them said, "You want us to believe you were in bed? It's broad daylight."

"I had just got off of a 72-hour hunt. Believe me I went nowhere but to bed when I got home." I looked at my captain. "What's this about?"

"The Vampire Council reported that one of their representative's Blood-Bond mate had been kidnapped and said one of our department sedans was the kidnap vehicle."

"And you thought of me. I'm flattered," I said sarcastically.

"Finn," my captain said warningly. "This is serious."

"No, it's not. If I was going to kidnap someone, I sure wouldn't use the department sedan and I surely wouldn't have done it in daylight where it would have been recognized. And if someone was stupid enough to become a slave to a vampire..." I broke off and shook my head. "Now I'm going to go upstairs and eat, then go back to bed."

The vampires made as if to protest but my captain threw them a look and they remained silent.

I pushed off from my car and headed to the stairway. Doors slammed and I heard the vehicles start before I made it up the stairs. This must have been what the winds had whispered to Cora. Words carried by the wind.

After unlocking the door, I stepped inside, then paused before closing the door behind me. "I didn't see either of your vehicles," I told them as I switched on the light. My apartment only had three windows, two of which were in the bedroom. "And the lock didn't look picked."

Louis and Doyle were sitting on my couch, drinking some of the beer I kept here for Louis the few times he came over.

"We came on my motorcycle," Louis told me. "I parked it behind the dumpster out back."

"And I got a touch with locks," Doyle said lazily.

I dropped into the chair and set the bag down on the coffee table before opening it. The smell caused my stomach to growl loudly. Both males laughed but I ignored them as I tore into the fast food. Even with the healing Cora had done, my mental and physical energy reserves were still low and the grease and calories would give me a huge boost. But only sleep would restore me fully. Uninterrupted sleep.

Louis waited until I was finished before he spoke again. "As soon as you left, they disengaged, and they and the two others went back around the building. I heard vehicles start up and tear out, but I figured you had a good enough head start."

"Would have been if they hadn't put a tracker on my car."

Doyle sat forward abruptly and looked at me but didn't say anything.

"What?" Louis exclaimed as he looked at me sharply himself.

"Yep." I made a dismissive gesture. "But those particular vampires are not a problem anymore. However it seems they were in contact with others."

"Your visitors in the parking lot?" Louis asked.

“It seems someone on the vampire council reported a Blood-Bond missing and the kidnapping vehicle as a department sedan.”

“You think that someone will try something?”

“What do you think?” I asked him wryly as creaking came from both my bedroom and outside my front door.

CHAPTER 3

Louis got up and strode over to the front door while Doyle moved on the couch to where he could see the bedroom door. My partner threw open my door and glared at the two vampires standing there.

The taller one straightened and inclined his head to Louis. "Citizen. May we enter?"

"Let them in, Louis," I said. "So their friends can get out of my bedroom."

My partner stepped aside but continued to glare at our two front visitors as they entered.

These two were not the two that had come with my captain. However, the two that came from my bedroom were. Doyle kept his eyes on the two from the bedroom while Louis stood near the other two.

"As I said before I went straight to bed when I got home."

"Your captain thought of you when we reported

the kidnapping," the vampire who had spoken before said.

I snorted. "My views on slavery are well known. However most of the detectives in SCD feel the same way. They just don't speak out, especially where the captain or the rest of the Brass could hear them." I glanced at the two from the bedroom. "As your friends can verify I don't have your slave. So take them with you and leave."

He stared at me for a moment, then gestured the other two toward the front door but he and his partner didn't move right away themselves. As the other two reluctantly headed for the door, he returned his eyes to me. "I will take your word for now. However ..."

"Don't say any more," I interrupted his threat. "You forget I'm a cop. This little visit of yours is enough to get you censored if I wanted. If you continue with your threat, I'd feel compelled to arrest you. Right now I'm too tired to want to do that. But I won't be next time. Now leave before my partner decides to throw you out."

Louis gave them a toothy smile.

The vampire inclined his head, then he and his partner joined the others at the front door. He gave us one last look before the four of them left.

"They'll be back," Doyle said.

"Not if they know what's good for them," my partner said as he made sure the door was locked.

"I'll renew the wards on the windows and door," I told them. "They won't be able to get in without me knowing and it'll weaken them."

Doyle raised an eyebrow.

“I'm not a damsel in distress. I can take care of myself.”

Vampires had an old fashion attitude toward females and a lot of the werewolves did too as there were not a lot of females compared to the males. Their gallantry was appreciated by many human women, but also irritated them too, especially when it became controlling.

The Lycan put his hands up in surrender and smiled.

“Why don't you make yourself useful and make sure they didn't leave any surprises like a bug in my bedroom?” I told him. When both Louis and him looked at me with raised eyebrows, I shrugged. “What's one more violation of my privacy?”

Doyle slid to his feet and went into my bedroom.

“I don't think you should be alone,” Louis said, frowning.

“You can't stay here forever, Louis,” I told him.

“I wasn't thinking of me,” he said. “Doyle caused this, he should take care of it.”

I frowned at him.

A gleam lit his eyes as he stared back at me.

I didn't like that look. Whatever caused that gleam I wanted nothing to do with, so I shook my head. “No. I'll be fine. As I said I can take care of myself.”

He snorted. “I could take you right now. Whatever happened after you left has drained you.”

I scowled at him. He knew me too well to be fooled, at least concerning my physical condition. Hopefully the other vampires hadn't picked up on my weakness or if they had they had contributed it to my lack of sleep for the past three days.

Doyle exited my bedroom and slouched on my couch. I knew better than to think he hadn't heard us talking, wolf ears after all. He tossed something at me, and I caught it.

It was a smashed bug.

“Only the one,” he said. “But doesn't mean they don't have a directional mic pointed this way.”

Luckily that wouldn't be a problem once I renew the wards.

Louis looked at me and I stared back.

“Not to break up this meaningful stare fest,” Doyle said. “But it's not a hardship for me to spend the night with a handsome woman.”

“I notice you didn't say beautiful,” I told him, looking away from Louis to him.

“You may not be what most humans would call beautiful, but I am not human.”

I stared at him, and Louis laughed. “Are you trying to flirt with me?” I asked incredulously.

“No. I don't think you are receptive to flattery. I think you hate it in fact.. I'm just stating facts.”

I didn't know what to say to that.

All my life I had been either the tomboy hanging out with my guy friends or the freak. I had never really dated or had that kind of relationship with anyone. Not that I hadn't had sex. Teenage weres were walking hormones and I had spent years with Cora and Walter. But no one had wanted to stay with the weird girl. Had he been a human male, I would know how to handle his advances with put downs and disdain for the obvious manipulation, but weres couldn't really fake interest. Oh they could flirt and be charming, but you could tell that that was all it was, not real interest. But Doyle's eyes showed his real interest, plus his words had confirmed it.

I scowled at my still smiling partner as he said, “You made her speechless. I didn't think that possible.” He was trying to relieve the suddenly tense atmosphere I knew, but I didn't appreciate his attempt right now.

“And I can also smell that you're not sexually attracted to either of us,” Doyle continued, ignoring my partner.

“It's not that I don't think you both are handsome, I just...”

“No need to explain,” he interrupted. “Some of us once past our hormonal puberty don't want the sex, just the intimacy of touch.”

“I knew,” Louis said quietly. “Our sense of smell may not be as developed as shifters', but we can tell when someone's interested. You obviously like my looks but no arousal smell and yet you are very tactile with me.”

I leaned forward and buried my face in my hands, my elbows on my knees. And here I had thought I had hidden myself well. Not that I was ashamed of myself but trying to fit in and keep things private. When the Others revealed themselves, attitudes toward many things changed but there were still remnants of old behaviors and attitudes among humans where sexual things were concerned. A lot voiced the politically correct opinion in public, however, in private or where they thought they could get away with dissent, that was another matter. I was weird enough without adding this.

"Calli." Louis squatted beside me and laid a hand on my leg. He rarely called me that, preferring to call me my proper name though he knew I hated it. "Calli," he said again.

I raised my head and looked at him.

"It's all right. If it makes you feel any better the other detectives and most of the uniforms think we're having kinky vampire sex."

"Oh, Mother," I muttered as I felt warmth sweep my cheeks.

Louis smiled. "And if Doyle drops by a few times, they'll probably think you're doing us both."

I gave him a half-hearted glare.

He patted my leg, then stood. "You'd best do those wards, then go to bed. We have to be in tomorrow morning to do the paperwork for the kidnapping case."

"And see if there's anything new on our other cases," I added, glad for the change of subject. "We let them lapse because of this case."

"Aye." He strode over to the door, then turned slightly and looked at Doyle. "Guard her well."

There was an implied threat in both his look and voice, but Doyle remained relaxed on the couch and just gave a little wave of his hand.

Louis wrinkled his nose, then opened the door. "I'll see you in the morning, Callista."

I gave him a little wave and he shook his head at me before he left, closing the door behind him. Gathering up my trash, I stood then carried it into the kitchen area where I tossed it into the trash can under the sink. The rest of my drink went into the refrigerator for later. I grabbed a small unlabeled jar off the countertop next to the sink and headed back into the living room area.

Doyle hadn't moved from his position on the couch. He had just turned his head to follow me.

The open style of the kitchen and living room suited me, though I wish this apartment had more windows for the natural light. But it did have an airy feel to it, even though it was small. And that was what I needed.

In a few more strides I was before the door. After making sure it was locked, I opened the jar and set the lid on the little table by the door. Holding the jar in one hand, I dipped my index finger of the other in the jar, then began drawing symbols on the door frame with the oil on that finger as I muttered the incantation of the ward. I had to dip many times to finish the ward and felt the drain as it took.

It wasn't magic as people think of magic, but a matter of will and intent. Putting a bit of oneself into something. Energy.

I repeated the ward at the window before heading into the bedroom.

My bed was between the two windows on the back wall where the fire escape was. Like the living room the bedroom had just the basics plus a TV sitting on the dresser. But each window here had a plant hanging in it, vines. The vampires had had to force their way through, and the vines were not happy.

I sent a burst of calm energy toward them, then started to draw the wards on the windows. Though I really didn't need the wards with the plants here as their upset would—and had—tell me of any intrusion through these windows. But better safe than sorry as they say.

After the last symbol and the bit of drain, I stepped back and allowed myself to relax for a second, feeling the exhaustion in my bones. The lack of sleep the last few days, the work of will at the farm, and the drawing of the wards were taking their toll, even with the bit of healing Cora had done. I had over done. Had Cora not been there I would probably have gone into a coma or even died. But I had to neutralize the danger I had caused, no matter how unwittingly. And I couldn't have fought all four at once, even with Walter's help. Cora would have tried to help too, exposing her. So...

Doyle cleared his throat and I looked toward the doorway. “Like the old saying says 'No use crying over spilt milk'.”

He had obviously sensed my downturn of mood and correctly guessed it's cause.

“Emotions aren't logical as you well know,” I told him as I turned and headed towards him.

“No, they aren't,” he agreed as he allowed me to brush by him.

I went to the front door and got the jar's lid, putting it on as I turned back into the room. Doyle had returned to the couch I saw and, tightening the lid, I headed into the kitchen to return the jar to its place on the counter. I glanced around and made sure everything was where it should be before heading toward my bedroom again. “You can leave the light on if you need to,” I told him as I paused in my doorway and looked back at him. “It won't bother me.”

He gave me a little wave.

I continued on into my bedroom and kicked off my shoes before flinging myself on the bed. With my luck I'd have visitors before morning, and I didn't want to be caught without my clothes if I had to fight. Not that I haven't or wouldn't, but my human sensibilities just made it mentally awkward. I was still human no matter my latter up-bringing. My exhaustion overwhelmed me just then, and I fell into deep sleep.

CHAPTER 4

A hand on my shoulder awoke me.

Doyle was standing by my bed. He withdrew his hand and took a step back when he saw I was awake.

"What time is it?" I asked as I sat up and rubbed my eyes. Most of my energy had been restored with the sleep but I was still tired physically.

"Just after dawn. I need to go. Your partner's on the way over."

I then noticed the phone in his other hand.

"Pack emergency," he said at my raised eyebrow. "I called Dufort afterwards."

I zipped into the bathroom for a pit stop and splashed some water on my face before I rejoined Doyle in my bedroom. "You think it may be a diversion?" I asked him as we walked into the living area.

He shrugged.

"Got up on the wrong side of the couch?"

He snorted but didn't answer as he headed for the door. Shifters took pack matters very seriously. Pack came before anything else, except for very rare instances.

I moved a chair until I could see both the front door and my bedroom door, then sat down. My gun had dug into me as I slept, however exhaustion had made it a non-issue, but now I rearranged it for better comfort--and draw.

"I'll call later," he said as he opened the door. Then he was gone before I could say anything.

It wasn't very long before there was a knock at my door. I knew it wasn't Louis as he would have just used his key. But being locked wouldn't stop them from entering I knew so I just said, "Come in."

Vampires didn't have to be invited in to enter but it did lessen their strength if they were not. They hadn't mention that to humans though of course, but the immortals had let that cat out of the bag. Nothing like rivalry to reveal secrets.

Two of the vampires from before entered. A ripple went through me as they passed my ward, but they didn't react at all, so they had not felt it. They stopped halfway between me and the door.

"I must ask you to come with us, Ms. Finn," the one vampire said.

"You have the advantage of knowing *my* name," I told him, ignoring the rest of his sentence for now.

"I am known as Barrett."

"Well, Barrett, I hope you won't be as

quarrelsome as your name suggests you are when I decline your offer."

Red flared in his companion's eyes but only humor glinted in Barrett's brown eyes. "It's an offer you can't really refuse."

Louis stepped out of my bedroom. He must have already been on his way here when Doyle had called him. I had felt him come through the window ward but had kept my attention on the vampires.

Barrett frowned. "Where is Mallory and Keres?"

"They're a bit tied up at the moment," Louis replied with a smile that was more a baring of teeth than a grin.

His companion took a step forward, but Barrett grabbed his arm and shook his head. The vampire hissed but stepped back.

"Mael Mrak wants to see her," Barrett said.

"Does he?" I asked. "Then he needs to stop hiding in my bedroom."

A cloaked figure stepped out of my bedroom. The older the vampire got the more sensitive they got to sunlight, but never to the point where they vaporize like Hollywood made it. But they did burn.

I had felt him cross the window ledge, causing my ward to collapse which had told me he was an Ancient. Ancient vampires were like sinqs, disrupting energy. Why, we, elementals, didn't know. It wasn't just age, because not all old vampires did this.

Raising his hands, the new visitor pushed his hood down. His black hair was pulled back into a ponytail and fell to his shoulders while dark eyes looked out of an androgynous yet weathered face.

"Vlad Dracula. Or should I call you Mael Mrak?"

He gave me what he probably thought was a charming smile, but I was too wary to trust anything about him. "You may call me either, Detective."

"Why would the Prince of Darkness want to see me?"

"Ah, straight to business." He took a step forward but stopped when Louis shifted. "I do not intend to hurt her, Dufort."

"What is intended and what actually happens isn't always the same thing," my partner told him.

Barrett's companion growled and took a step toward Louis, but again Barrett pulled him back.

Vlad frowned and looked at Barrett. "Why don't you take Silas back to the car," he told the vampire. "And when you're done, release the others."

Barrett and Vlad seemed to be communicating with their eyes for a moment before Barrett nodded and led his companion outside, closing the door behind them.

"Trouble among the ranks?" I asked not expecting an answer.

"Yes," Vlad replied. "Which is why I'm here."

He looked and felt sincere.

"It has come to my attention that certain fractions among my people have been doing things they shouldn't. I traced one such thing to this city."

"I don't mean to be harsh, but what does it matter to you? You abdicated and abolished the King of Vampires thing long ago when your Others came out. And let's face it you don't have a very good reputation."

"True on both accounts. However, I don't wish all my people to be judged and punished by the actions of just one group."

"You sure it's just a fraction or group?" I asked. "It seems quite a lot of you vampires hunt Elementals from what I have seen and heard."

"Most of them lived during the time when the Justices had begun their reign. They were suddenly held accountable for their actions. Which of course they didn't like but couldn't do anything about then. But now, well." He shrugged. "The human ambivalence about Elementals suits them just fine."

"They should have been reined in before that," I told him.

Vlad bowed his head in acknowledgment but didn't offer any excuses for his lack.

"You said you followed an incident here?" Louis asked, obviously trying to change the subject at least a bit.

"Yes. I plan to fix the problem here. However, I want to ensure more do not crop up. Which is why I'm here. I need someone to 'police' the vampire community here, someone who is not mixed up with them and can't be bribed."

"The Council will not allow that. They already chaff under the Charter."

"They'll have no choice," Vlad said in a grim voice.

"Wait," Louis said. "You want Calista to be that someone? Is that what you're saying?"

"Who better than a Justice of the Peace?"

I looked at the Ancient sharply.

"Fear not, Calista Finn." Vlad held up his hands

in peace. “Didn't you ever wonder why some ancient vampires are sinqs? We were Elementals in life before our change and we can still recognize our old kind.”

I frowned. That could be problematic depending upon the Ancient.

Barrett came in through my bedroom. My plants had told me when he had slipped through them. He stopped beside Vlad and straightened his clothing.

Louis's nose flared and he frowned, making me realize he smelled blood.

However before either of us could say anything, the front door opened, and Doyle stepped in.

“Please close the door, Mr. Doyle,” Vlad said.

Doyle closed the door behind him and moved to the couch where he coiled, his eyes on Vlad and Barrett.

“As I was saying I need an outside force to 'police' the vampire community here. They have already shown they cannot do it themselves.”

“And I told you they won't go for it.,” I repeated. “Once you leave they'll ignore or kill this 'force'.”

“Am I right that Mr. Doyle knows your secret?” Vlad asked me. When I nodded he turned his attention to Doyle. “Am I also right that she and Dufort don't know any of yours, Mr. Doyle?” The vampire obviously took Doyle's silence as conformation and turned back to me. “Doyle's grandmother was an Elemental, a healer to be exact.”

“Was?” I asked. Elementals could live quite a long time for humans, not as long as immortals of course, but longer than normal. Of course humans lived longer now anyways with the advances the Others had brought to the medical system. But Elementals rarely took advantage of that health system due to fear of discovery.

"Vampires caught her out alone one night," Doyle said. "Don't know if they knew she was an Elemental or were just careless. They received a slap on the wrist."

"They also disappeared one by one," Barrett spoke up as he eyed Doyle. "No sign of them was ever found."

Doyle kept his expression neutral as he returned Barrett's look.

"So he already keeps an eye on the local vampires," Louis commented.

"Yes. However, I've found that a more visible and authorized force is necessary to curve this fraction and the arrogance of the Councils."

"So an official force," Louis said in an even voice. He wasn't making it a question.

"In a way," Vlad told him. "You can keep your day jobs but when needed you would take this up."

"Why do I have the feeling we don't really have a choice in this?" I asked.

Vlad smiled.

I didn't like the look of that smile. It told me I was right.

"Mael Mrak has re-instated the rector post," Barrett said. "You would say provost, I believe."

"And those two would be your guard." Vlad made a gesture toward Louis and then Doyle. "As would Barrett."

"I'm a detective with the police not your personal

enforcer," I protested.

"Nor do I expect you to be," Vlad's dark eyes met mine. "As I have said you would still be working your day jobs, just when the vampires step out of line you will have the authority to drag them back."

Doyle snorted. "Once you leave that authority would be gone with you. And we'd have targets on our backs."

"You already had that," Barrett said. "The fraction had some members who planned to pay you and your personal pack a visit."

His eyes narrowed as the shifter looked at Barrett.

"Ah, that's why you left," Barrett concluded. "I guess I missed a few then." He gave Doyle a toothy grin that made me suspect he had missed the few on purpose.

Vlad gave Barrett a look and growled, a warning clear in his tone, "Barrett."

The vampire tilted his head, but I could tell Barrett wasn't sorry or abashed at all. "Still," I said. "Doyle is correct. The Council would not allow a mere human any authority like that much less let a Lycan corral them. Especially without your coercion."

"They have and will," Vlad said, then added, "And I suspect that that is the head of the Council out there."

Doyle had turned his head toward the door and was now growling in a low tone.

"Since she wouldn't come with us," Barrett said. "I made a call while I was out."

Vlad shook his head and sighed, in exasperation it sounded like to me.

“That isn't your head of Council out there,” Doyle said in a growling voice, just as the front door was slammed open and I felt intruders burst through my bedroom windows.

CHAPTER 5

Doyle didn't take the time to transform. He merely launched himself at the bear lumbering toward us as the three vampires turned and flew toward the two bears coming out of my bedroom. Louis and Barrett attacked one while Vlad took on the other. Doyle got a strangle hold and forced his bear to the floor where she shifted into human form before she became unconscious. The vampires wrestled theirs to the floor before they too shifted to human form, still struggling in the vampires' grips.

I recognized the female and two young males. They were the younger siblings of the shifter who had kidnapped the child we had just rescued. I stood and went over to the female who was just regaining consciousness. Her bare body was slick with the viscous clear fluid of reverse change and hair covered the floor. She had been the one who suggested this I was sure and talked the males into it.

Doyle held her down with a foot between her shoulder blades, but she managed to glare up at me.

"Because of your actions here," I told her. "Your whole clan pack could be Censored."

"Like you weren't going to do that anyway!" She spit that out angrily, then yelped as Doyle leaned down and slapped her across the head.

"Doyle," I said.

The shifter relented and let up on the pressure on her shoulder blades, allowing her to breathe better.

"Only Sandy would have been Censored for her actions, though your clan pack would have faced citations for their interference."

"That's not what Sandy said," she exclaimed.

"Did she tell you to come here?"

She didn't answer right away, and Doyle leaned a little on her. "She said without you and your partner they'd have to drop the charges as there'd be no proof."

"How did you even see her?" Louis asked, not even breathing hard from holding the still struggling young bear shifter. "Only her lawyer is supposed to be allowed to see her."

Again she didn't answer right away, and Doyle added pressure to her shoulder blades. "I convinced the guard I was one of the assistant lawyers."

Louis looked at the pretty, young female shifter. "And they believed you?"

She smirked. "I can be very convincing."

I snorted, then looked at my angry partner. "Leave it, Louis."

He made a face but nodded.

I turned my attention back to the female. “Your name's Oni, right?”

She tensed but didn't answer.

“That's becoming a habit with you.” I crossed my arms as I stared at her. She was probably the youngest and somewhat sheltered. At least that was what I suspected from what my gift was giving me. “Does your clan pack leader even know you're here?”

When she just stared at me, Doyle growled, “Answer her!”

“No,” she said with defiance clear in her voice.

“He does now,” Louis said. He had handed off the now still bear shifter to Barrett while I had been talking to the female and was now waving his phone. “I texted him. He said he'd be here soon.”

“What's going on here?” Came a familiar voice from the doorway.

Our captain was standing there with two beings looking over his shoulders. One was a black woman in a matching skirt and blazer I recognized as our new Commissioner Elena Davis and the other was a vampire that was no doubt the head of the vampire Council.

“Just a misunderstanding,” I answered. “Which will be straightened out pretty soon.”

“Looks like more than just a misunderstanding,” our captain said.

“I agree,” said the Commissioner as she stepped around our captain and entered my apartment. “Was this what I was asked here for?”

“No, Commissioner Davis,” Vlad said. “This is

as Finn says just a misunderstanding."

The vampire and our captain entered and stood with the Commissioner near the door as three others came up to my door. I recognized one of them as the clan pack leader Cristo.

"You made it here quickly," I commented.

"I was not far away when your partner texted," Cristo said as he stepped into my apartment, leaving his two pack members at the door. He stood over Oni and glared down at her, but she wouldn't meet his eyes. "What do you have to say for yourself, young one?"

"You let them take her!" she spit out.

"She broke the law and if we hadn't *we* would have been the ones Censored. And now thanks to you we may well be." He looked at me. "All I can say is that she is young and spoiled. Much like Sandy was."

"I know females are rare in your clan pack, Clan Leader Cristo," I told him. "And I do not want to deprive you of another, but I cannot just let this go."

"I understand." He sighed.

"However..." I paused. "In both our societies we have what we humans call community service where instead of jail time the being does work assigned to improve public or community areas. While I know the members of a clan work towards improvement of the clan anyway, I know you also have something similar."

"Yes."

"If you promise to assign her at least two-hundred hours, worth of this work, this will go no further. Understand I'm releasing her into your custody and you're responsible for insuring she does the work. Otherwise, I will push this further."

"I understand." He reached down and grabbed Oni's arm, then pulled her up when Doyle removed his foot from between her shoulder blades. "You may release the males, vampires. They won't cause any more problems."

As soon as they were released the young males headed for the door with their heads down where the other two shifters grabbed an arm.

"All three of them shall do 'community service', but she shall do more of it as she instigated it. Thank you for your compassion and understanding." He dragged Oni to the door, then he and the other bear shifters left.

"I had reservations about your proposal," the head of the vampire Council said to Vlad. "And while I still have them I'm more inclined to believe it will work."

"Proposal?" the Commissioner asked. "And who are you?"

"I'm Lucian, head of the Council." He gave a slight bow to her.

"I thought Atieno was head of the vampire Council."

"There's been a bit of change." Vlad gave her a slight smile. "And that's part of the reason you were asked here."

"This proposal Lucian mentioned?"

"Yes." He inclined his head in a slight nod.

"Why are we having this discussion here? Wouldn't one of our offices be better?"

"That was our original plan," Barrett said with a

look at me.

I returned to my chair and sat while Doyle and Louis moved to stand behind me and present a united front. Barrett wasn't going to make me regret not going with him earlier. I didn't trust him further than I could physically throw him. Which was not very far as vampires and shifters were heavier than mundanes due to muscle composition, so science said. I just knew they were heavy.

"In our society there was a position called Rector," Vlad said. "You humans would call it Provost, though it didn't have quite the same outreach as that job. He or she had almost unlimited power in investigating and judging criminal activity among the Upire. Only the King was the higher judge. The position has been empty since the last Rector retired and we have been merged with human society."

"We shifters have something similar in our larger packs," Doyle said as Vlad paused. "Enforcers carry out the Council's commands instead of a single leader's now, but disputes and other things are still judged by the—Provost. I am the Provost for the Lycan of this city."

"What about the Councils?" the Commissioner asked. "I thought that was part of their job."

"For the vampire Council it was so," Vlad said. "But some problems have shown themselves and we are re-instating the position of Rector or Provost as it will now be called. This Provost and her three Guards or assistants as you would call them would be the liaison between the Council and your police and would do the investigation concerning anything

Upire."

The Commissioner frowned.

"It is accounted for in the Charter," Barrett told her. "I can send you an email with that information if you like."

"I would, thank you."

"I'll tell you straight up that I think this is a bad idea," our captain said. "Finn doesn't have a diplomatic bone in her body." Our captain wasn't a stupid man by any means and had put everything together to come up with the correct inference.

The Commissioner transferred her gaze to me.

"Thanks for the vote of confidence, Captain," I said sarcastically.

He shrugged. "You know I don't sugar coat the truth."

"I'm well aware of her faults," Vlad said with obvious humor in his voice and a gleam in his eyes. "However she is perfect for this."

"If you want conflict," our captain retorted.

"Why her?" the Commissioner asked.

"I see the fire within."

I gave him a sharp look. Fire indeed had to do with judgment, but it was hardly my motivating factor, my job notwithstanding. I was Earth, balanced with Water. So maybe I was fit for the job. After all balance may be what he was after, not just judgment.

"I will need to look over that section of the Charter before *I* can agree to anything," the Commissioner said. "I gather you want me to inform the rest of the city council and the Mayor about this?"

"Yes," Lucian spoke for the first time since this discussion began. "I will want to ratify this at the full monthly meeting."

"I'll send all the relative information and paperwork in the email," Barrett interjected.

"Thank you." The Commissioner gave him a nod, then looked back at Lucian. "And if it is not ratified?"

"As far as the vampire Council is concerned she is already the Provost," Lucian told her.

"I see." She looked over to Doyle. "And your stance on this?"

"On this issue I am in accord with the vampire Council."

Her eyebrows went up. I'm sure in surprise as the Lycan hardly ever sided with the vampires on anything. "And the shifter Council as a whole?"

He gave her a smile with lots of teeth. "There will be a lot of discussion."

"Then I'm glad I won't be there. But I'll warn the Mayor at least."

Doyle gave her a slight nod.

She turned her attention back to me. "You haven't really said anything, Detective."

"What's there to say?" Louis laid his hand on my shoulder, a warning I'm sure not to say anything *he'd* regret as I'm also sure he heard the underlying frustration and touch of anger in my tone. Barrett had said it was an offer I couldn't refuse, and they had insured that. I didn't mind the job as it was needed but I would have like to have had at least an illusion of a say in the matter.

She studied my face, but I knew my poker face

was good. Had to be, really, with my secrets. After a moment she turned her attention away from me and toward Vlad. "I've met everyone on the vampire Council, yet I don't know you and I should, given the way Lucian deferred to you."

"I'm Mael Mrak, Council to the Council." Vlad gave her a slight bow. "You would call me a Fixer in modern vernacular."

I was surprised he told her that. He was being almost up front with her. What he was doing would indeed fit in a Fixer's job for the most part but the whys and wherefores were different.

"The problems mentioned?"

Vlad inclined his head.

"To require a Fixer is a major thing," she stated. "Especially when it involves the changing of the head of the Council. Should we be concerned?"

"It has been taken care of," Barrett said. His tone held enough firmness to say nothing more was going to be said about this.

The Commissioner looked at Lucian, but he merely stared back at her.

I could tell she was frustrated but it really wasn't any of her business. Humans may be the majority but that didn't give humans the right to butt into Other's business--especially not to tell them how to handle it or what to do. I realize the irony for the job I was to do a Provost, but still she didn't have the right to stick her nose in. Policing was one thing, butting in was another.

"Perhaps we should see if we can catch the Mayor before his first appointment," our captain said. As I said he wasn't stupid, and no doubt felt the tension in the air. Nobody wanted this to turn hostile.

The Commissioner stared at Lucian a moment longer, then straightened a bit and turned her attention to our captain. "That sounds like a good idea. Gentlemen," she said with a little nod before turning and heading for my front door.

"My office," our captain said to me before he followed the Commissioner out.

I was not looking forward to that meeting.

"Do not let them dis-sway you," Vlad said. "We were self-governing before we revealed ourselves. Perhaps the years have dulled the memories of our races. Human memory is short so I can understand their forgetting of things, but there is no excuse for the rest of us."

"I don't believe that is the whole problem," I told him. "Your people have ever been arrogant and there has always been those who believe the rest of us are beneath them. They have I believe united. And combined with the rareness of Elementals and the open ambivalence toward them, those beings have gained both the power and courage to move."

"As I said they have forgotten how things were," Vlad said. "I'm tempted to remind them myself, but Barrett and a few others tell me that that would be disastrous for the relationship we have with the humans and disrupt our alliances."

"A wholesale killing spree would indeed do that." I noticed the look between Vlad and Barrett. "A few killings, properly disposed off is one thing. But wholesale slaughter is another, especially with your reputation."

"The humans wouldn't know it was me."

Both Doyle and I snorted while the three other vampires shot him a look.

"Okay, okay." Vlad held his hands up in surrender for a moment then dropped them. "However if I have to, I will. My people have strayed from the natural laws that were set forth as have some of the shifters and to a lesser extent the Immortals. The humans may be ignorant of them but we Others are not. At least we were not. You will remind them. And much more nicely then I will if they keep straying."

"No pressure," I muttered.

Barrett gave me an amused look while Lucian frowned at Vlad who met his eyes.

"I told you my thoughts on this," Vlad said.

"You said..."

"I said that this was the Council's second chance," Vlad told him. "That the Provost would be my voice in this. That I am staying my hand. But all this did not mean I would continue to do so if things were not corrected. And what I have done to give you this chance will pale in comparison should I need to rectify this myself."

"You really shouldn't be talking about this in front of police officers," I said. 'Suspecting' something and 'knowing' are two different things, especially in human law. There were a lot of differences in the Others' laws and human law which is why there was a Charter, to compromise and make the laws more universal. Do as you will as long as it harms no other was not a universal law with the Others. It wasn't even universal among humans before the Others revealed themselves. Still wasn't to tell the truth or there wouldn't be a need for SCD or even the regular police.

Vlad just flashed me a smile and Barrett gave me another amused look. They obviously knew I wasn't going to do anything with this information.

Lucian however straightened almost inappreciably. “You are correct. We should not be airing this in front of you.” He looked at Vlad. “Meet you back at the council chambers?”

“Actually, would you give me a ride? Barrett has an errand he needs to run.”

Yeah, I thought. Disposing of the three vampires he's killed this morning.

“Of course.” He turned to me. “I'll be in touch, Detective.”

“Okay.”

Vlad flashed me another smile, then he and Lucian left by the front door.

“I'll have one of my cubs come over and fix that door,” Doyle said as he pulled out his phone.

“We need to head into the station,” Louis said, glancing at the clock on my wall.

I made a face as I really wasn't looking forward to the meeting with our captain.

“Best to get it over with,” Louis told me.

“I'm coming with you,” Doyle said as he slide his phone back where it belonged.

From his tone and the gleam in his eyes I could tell arguing wouldn't get us anywhere, so I just stood. “Let's go then. We can stop at a drive-thru on the way.”

The two males fell in step behind me as I headed

to the door. Hopefully today wouldn't be as bad as I feared.

CHAPTER 6

The meeting started as bad as I feared. Our captain wasn't the only one in his office. The Commissioner was there too.

Louis and I sat in the chairs in front of our captain's desk with Doyle standing behind and between us. My partner was his inscrutable self while Doyle had on his 'open' face as if he didn't know why we were here. However, I was scowling.

"Finn," our captain said in a warning tone.

"I'm not going to use the position to further any political or personal agendas," I said, ignoring his warning.

"I wouldn't ask you to," the Commissioner said right away.

"Only because Doyle is here," I told her. "I caught the look on your face when he entered before you slid into your politically correct face."

“I saw it too,” Doyle said as the Commissioner opened her mouth, no doubt to deny it.

She closed her mouth and stared at us with a blank face for a moment before saying, “Surely with all of us working so closely together we should talk so we are all on the same page.”

“First of all there is no 'all of us' working together,” Doyle told her. “You are not wanted or needed beyond your ability to facilitate this smoothly. Second, the Charter makes sure we're all 'on the same page'.”

Her lips tightened and I could feel the anger and frustration radiating off her.

“I would advise you to read the email Barrett is sending you very carefully and thoroughly,” he added. “And make sure the Mayor gets a copy. We don't want any 'misunderstandings', do we?”

“No.” Her words were abrupt. “I set up a meeting with the Mayor for over lunch so he will be at least briefed today. When I get the email, I will send a copy along to him.”

“Excellent.”

“Captain.” The Commissioner nodded to our captain who nodded back before she headed to the door.

Our captain waited until the door closed behind her before he spoke. “I see Finn isn't the only one without a political bone.”

“Oh, I can be diplomatic,” Doyle said. “But beings like that, who put political or personal agendas first, piss me off.”

So it would for pack animals. The pack came first, not individuals. Though that didn't mean they didn't care or defend the individual. Just that the whole came first, then the individual. You didn't screw over your pack--or partner.

"Can we get back to work now?" I asked. "We still got cases open that we had to put aside for the kidnapping."

"And the paperwork for the kidnapping case," our captain said. "I know you didn't do any of it yet."

I made a face, then looked at Louis and raised an eyebrow.

He rolled his eyes. "Yes, I'll do it."

Our captain shook his head at us, then gestured to the door. "Get out of here."

Louis and I stood and walked to the door, but Doyle plopped down in one of the chairs in front of the desk. I looked back at him. "Doyle?"

"I need to have a chat with your captain. I'll stop by your desks before I leave."

I stared at him a moment, but I wasn't getting anything from him, so I nodded, and Louis and I left the office. We glanced around the busy squad room, then head for our desks near the 'front' of the bullpen.

The basement had four double doors leading into our area, but only two lead to the building's two elevators while one lead toward the record and property rooms and the other to stairs. One part of the stair went up to the side alley and the other went up all the way to the roof. All the desks were situated in a T shape, supposedly better for our mental health and more visually appealing in our little dungeon of an area, and made of metal with a fake wood top, also supposedly good for our mental attitude. To also keep us 'happy' they designated the door that lead to the main elevator as the 'front' of the bullpen. I hadn't notice that any of this had kept our attitudes 'up'. We were still who we were and doing a thankless job that other cops, detectives, didn't want to do.

We slid into our chairs as soon as we reached our desks. I straightaway turned to my computer, but Louis didn't immediately get on his and I looked sideways at him. He was staring at me, and I raised an eyebrow.

"Are you really alright with this?"

"While I would not have chosen this path myself," I told him. "I am not opposed to following it."

"That's not really an answer."

But that was all he was going to get from me on the subject, at least while we were in the station. I gave him a shrug and turned back to my computer.

Louis stared at me for a few more seconds then got on his own computer.

The kidnapping had taken us away from three cases, two of which were murders. Luckily we were now at the bottom of the rotation and had time to work on them. Unless of course I was called in as Provost.

This new gig could get irritating fast.

Doyle glided up to our desks with his usual animal grace and propped himself against mine. "I'm your new consultant."

I gave him a sharp look but all he did was give me a smile.

Louis was frowning at him.

"I told you when we first met, that this was the beginning of a wonderful relationship."

Bonus Drabble
A Killing Wind
The Meeting

You'd think in a world full of vampires, shifters and immortals, a person who could control the elements would fit right in.

But you'd be wrong.

It seems nobody likes witches. Or the supernatural. Vampirism, lycanthropy, and immortality can all be explained scientifically through viruses and DNA, but elementals—it can't be quantified. So it's something to be feared by humans. There are no actual laws against elementals, but some are slanted that way.

With that you'd also think that if you were one of these elementals, you'd stay away from law enforcement so you wouldn't be tagged.

Well, you'd be wrong there too, at least in my case. Detective Calli Finn of the Lansdell Police Department, Special Circumstances Division at your service.

SCD handles all the crimes where the vampires, shifters, or immortals are involved. You could say I sort of fell into the job. Which most of the detectives in this division could say. No one volunteers for this assignment. This division has the most casualties of the whole department, and you make a lot of high-powered enemies. But it needs to be done.

My partner Louis and I are the next up on rotation. We still have three open cases, but we just closed one. I lucked out on the partner bit, not only is he good-looking with his All-American blond-haired, blue-eyed look but he's a damn fine detective. Next to him I look like a mousy nerd in jeans.

Louis' phone rang and he answered with "Dufort."-

I straightened and shoved the file I had been looking at away. By the frown on his face it wasn't good. "Sooo?" I asked as he hung up.

"Bodies in Korrigan Park." He stood and grabbed his weapon from his drawer as he spoke.

The park he named was the main park in the city. It was neutral territory. Bodies there were definitely not good. I stood and grabbed my gun as well before following him to the bullpen door. I felt the eyes on us. The few female detectives were eyeing Louis like he was a steak they craved. Most vampires gave off sexual vibes, part of their lure to get your blood, but not a lot of them were as good-looking as Louis. Louis of course just ignored them.

So maybe I am the one with the problem about them.

We left the bullpen and headed down the hall to the elevator. SCD was in the basement, of course. While well-enough funded, it was not popular or a priority. Humans were still at the top of the heap at killing and other violent crimes.

"They didn't give you any details?" I asked as we rode the elevator up to the lobby.

"No."

That was unusual in itself. And further told me it was definitely bad.

We stepped out into chaos. The lobby was full of people and the front desk was besieged. Louis grabbed my arm and bulldozed our way through to the front door. We would be coming in the back way when we returned.

Once outside, Louis let go of my arm and we hurried to where we had parked this morning. That tidbit about vampires burning in the sunlight is pure Hollywood, same about wolf shifters and the full moon. A lot of myths were found untrue when the vampires, shifters, and immortals came out all those years ago.

I slid into the driver's seat before Louis could. His driving was terrible. He took the rules as suggestions. As soon as Louis was settled, I pulled out into traffic and headed toward the park.

Korrigan Park was indeed neutral territory for the Others, as we humans unofficial call the vampires, shifters, and immortals as a whole. It was the largest park in the city and was situated almost virtually in the center of the city. Woods and trails covered most of it, though there were a few grassy areas at its perimeters and along some paths. The shifters used it a lot when they wanted 'animal time' and when the two other wooded parks were occupied whether by humans or other shifter clans. Knowing it's a shifter and seeing a huge predator up close are two different things. And predator animals don't get along with other predatory animals, even if they have higher-functioning brains controlling them.

It didn't take long to get to the park. I turned into the half-full parking lot and pulled alongside one of the patrol units. Louis and I got out of the car and glanced around.

Uniforms and CSU were moving about the grassy area and into the woods. A group had congregated near the standalone wrought iron gate that marked the entrance to the park. I recognized the white-haired M.E. and her young assistants in the group as well as our Captain but the other two I didn't know. However, I could tell they were vampires. My gift told me that much, even though I was standing on asphalt and they on concrete.

Due to their nature the Others were more connected to the Earth element than humans and I could sense them. Came in handy in a chase or fight, let me tell you. Can't sneak up on me or evade me. Well, most of the time. Stone, asphalt, concrete and other man-made things interfered with my gift.

Our captain saw us just then and waved us over.

The M.E.'s assistants headed off toward their van as we joined the group.

"You know Dr. Collins," our captain said as he gestured to her.

We nodded to the elderly M.E., then looked at the two vampires. Louis, I'm sure, knew they were vamps. They had a special sense of each other.

"This is Mr. Abaddon and Mr. Apollyon from the vampire council. We are awaiting a member of the shifter council."

Louis quirked his lips. I'm sure he found their names amusing as did I, though I hoped it didn't bode evil for our case to have ruin and destroyer as compatriots.

To investigate these crimes we had to get co-operation from the councils or things went awry. People were suddenly not available. Evidence disappeared. Information dried up. Didn't mean we couldn't do our jobs, just that it was easier if we got the councils co-operation.

And since we needed both councils' co-op, that meant either there were at least two bodies, or the killer was one kind and the victim the other. Louis and I would find out soon enough.

A short, stocky man with dark hair joined us. He was not dressed in a suit like the two vampires were but wore jeans and a button-down. Male shifters weren't fussy about their clothing or their looks, though some of them were ruggedly handsome like this guy. Made us humans seem drab and self-conscious by comparison.

The two vampires hissed and stepped back from the shifter who gave them a toothy smile.

By the reaction, I can guess that the shifter is a Lycan or a wolf shifter as vamps and Lycan hate each other. The other shifter clans don't like the vamps either, but the vamps have a rather tumultuous relationship with the Lycan. No human seems to know why, or it would have been all over the tabloids. Humans love their gossip, especially about the Others.

“Gentlemen, we are here about our victims, not personal feuds,” our captain said.

“Quite right, Captain Roberts,” the shifter said. “I'm Doyle.”

“This is Detective Finn and Detective Dufort.” We nodded to them, then the captain gestured to the gate. “Shall we?” The captain led the way under the gate and along the gravel path into the woods.

I was getting interesting impressions even though the gravel muffled the connection a bit. Several vampires and shifters had come this way recently, all headed in. None of them had returned this way. The impressions grew darker and violent the closer we came to the crime scene. Something had attacked the vampires and shifters and killed them. I couldn't see who it was, but I could feel him. Hatred radiated from his inner being.

The captain stopped and I moved around him to look at the scene.

Broken bodies lay strewn about. It looked as if a giant had flung the bodies against the trees. But the heads were what bothered me. They had all been taken off the bodies and lined up along the pathway. Decapitation was one sure way to kill any of the Others.

Doyle moved to one of the bodies and squatted. He sniffed the neck area, then looked around at the other bodies. “None of them shifted. Why wouldn't they?” He seemed to be talking more to himself than to any of us.

The two vampires also went over to a body and knelt to study it. They suddenly stood and moved back over to the captain, but they didn't say anything.

“Do we have your full co-operation with this investigation?” the captain asked.

“Yesss,” hissed both vampires. I could feel their anger—and their fear.

“Yes.” Doyle stood. “But I would like to tag along.”

I looked at him sharply. Was he looking for revenge? Did he know these shifters? Shifters were notorious about retribution. But his eyes were a warm brown, not yellow so he was not moved by strong emotion.

Our captain also looked at him sharply.

"This case intrigues me," he told our captain. "I am not looking to avenge. I knew none of these shifters."

"Alright." Our captain then turned to the M.E. "Doc."

"From my preliminary examination I can say they have various broken bones consistent with being thrown forcefully against a tree. The heads were cut then sawed off. I would suspect a serrated blade from what I could see of the markings. And I didn't see any defensive wounds. That's all I can tell until I do an autopsy."

"Thank you, Doctor. You can remove the bodies now."

Dr. Collins nodded and stepped away.

"These are the names on their Ids." Our captain pulled out three pieces of paper from his suit pocket and handed one to Louis before giving one to the vampires and the other to Doyle. "Three vampires and four shifters."

"None of which fought back according to your M.E." Doyle said as he glanced over the paper. "And the shifters didn't shift."

"Maybe they didn't have time," I said. The impressions I got told me it was fast, what had happened here. Cutting the heads would have taken time, but the initial attack had been fast. I still didn't get anything definitive, but I could extrapolate. “Something lured them here and disabled them before they could do anything.”

“That's how I see it,” Louis agreed.

Doyle scanned the paper with his phone and sent a text while the vampires muttered to each other. The vamps didn't seem happy and appeared to be arguing. I was suddenly unhappy myself; my gut was telling me they were hiding something. Something important.

Our captain frowned. “Gentlemen, is there something you want to tell us?”

The vampires shook their heads, but neither reached for a phone. Though they did stop arguing.

“It seems to me you know something about either these victims or the situation,” Our captain said. So he must have had that feeling too.

Doyle looked up from his phone and eyed the vampires.

“Fachnan and Mal were consultants to the council,” the one who called himself Ruin said reluctantly. “Keir we don't know.”

“By consultants you mean enforcers,” Louis said. The vampires gave him a sharp look, but Louis ignored that as he stared them down. “Who were they after?”

“There's been rumors of an elemental,” Ruin said almost unwillingly. “They were checking them out.”

Our captain frowned but didn't speak. He seemed to sink into his thoughts.

An elemental. And one off his rocker, judging by this scene. Was he truly crazy or was he exacting revenge was the question. Either way he was way too dangerous to leave alone and free.

We all watched as the bodies and heads were removed and the scene vacated by the CSU. Once everything was quiet, our captain cleared his throat. “I don't know why you vampires are so against elementals, and I don't care. But being one is not a crime. If we humans were as intolerant as you vampires are toward the elementals you Others would be the Hunted.”

“Not all of us are that way,” Louis said. “Just those in the Old Guard, as you would say.”

“If you knew the truth, you would be too,” the vampire who called himself Destroyer said in a harsh voice. “They are dangerous as you can see.”

“So are you,” I told him.

He shut up and just glared at me. After all he couldn't dispute my words.

“You will give my detectives the information they ask as per the Charter, or we will enact Clause 56.”

The Charter was the Other's constitution and bill of rights pertaining to living in a human dominated world. And there were consequences for both sides should someone violate the laws and rights contained within. Clause 56 concerned the vampires specifically.

Both vampires grimaced.

Whether from the threat or from having to tell us what they knew, I didn't know. But I got straight to the questioning before they could argue. “When did you hear from them last?”

“Last night around 8.” Ruin answered readily

enough but I could tell he wasn't going to volunteer anything.

“That's when Deimos called his girlfriend to tell her, he and the boys were going for a run,” Doyle said. “She called when he didn't come home by dawn.”

“Do you know what Fachnan, and Mal said?” I asked the vampires.

“Yes.” Ruin paused, then reluctantly continued when I raised an eyebrow at him. “Mal said they were on to something and were going to follow the lead.”

“And he didn't say what the lead was?” Louis asked.

I could tell he thought they were holding back. Hell, I knew they were.

Destroyer's jaw tightened and he crossed his arms over his chest when Ruin answered truthfully. “They thought they had found the elemental and were going to follow him.”

Our captain glared at them.

“That explains why the two enforcers were here, but what about the others?” Doyle asked. “The other vampire and the shifters. What had they to do with the elemental?”

“Perhaps the wrong place at the wrong time,” I said. Which could be true. If the elemental went all lure to draw in the enforcers who were following him the others might have been caught too. But they deserved more than being collateral damage if that was the case.

“Do you have any more questions for these 'gentlemen'?” our captain asked. When Louis, then I shook our heads, he gestured for the vampires to head back toward the cars. “Then I'll accompany them back. Take your time, Detectives. Representative Doyle.” He gave the shifter a nod, then escorted the vampires away.

“They're enforcers I take it?” I commented to Louis.

“Yes.” His answer was short. “Do your thing,” he told me just as abruptly.

Louis knew that I could read the ground. But he thought part of it was my tracking skills from being raised in the country and part psychometric reading. Many psychic powers were considered 'acceptable' as they had been proven in studies, so it was unobjectionable to normal humans and the Others. The vampires were especially against anything that smelled of 'magic'.

I stepped off the gravel pathway. The impressions became more vivid but no less confusing. There was still no clear picture of the perp, but I didn't expect one since he was an elemental. We were indistinct to one another when we used our gifts. I did get a faint trail though, leading deeper into the wood.

Doyle slipped his phone back into his pocket, then studied the ground himself.

My eyes still on the ground, I wandered a bit but generally toward where the trail tugged. I had to be careful with the Lycan here. Even though he seemed to be looking at the ground, I still caught him glancing toward me.

A bit of bloody cloth, really nothing more than a few pieces of thread, was caught on a bush and I moved closer as if to study it. “He went this way,” I said to draw them over.

Both Doyle's and Louis' noses flared as they joined me. Enhanced senses were part and parcel with both vampires and shifters, though shifters more so because of their animal aspect.

Doyle suddenly lunged forward into the wood, and Louis and I went after him.

Next thing I knew I was flung against a tree. I fell to the ground, then struggled to my feet and glanced around.

Doyle was slumped against a tree and Louis was in the middle of a windstorm. Leaves were whirling around him, then he went flying into a tree. The leaves swirled away from him and hovered in a whirlwind, but he didn't move. Seemingly satisfied that Louis was out for the count the wind creature headed toward me.

A young man was leaning against a tree, watching the action. He must be the elemental. Short and thin he didn't look like much but he had already proven he was dangerous.

“Graund!” I called.

Dirt and grass flew up into the air and solidified into a vaguely humanoid form. It stood between me and the leaf tornado creature.

The perp had a surprised look on his face.

Then I could feel him trying to lure me, to draw me to him. I took a step toward him and caught the flash of the blade in his hand but continued slowly toward him.

He was smiling.

But that smile dropped from his face when I

stopped just out of his reach. I felt the strength of the draw increase, but I just stood there, staring at him.

His eyes narrowed as he stared back, and a line appeared across his forehead. Obviously, he had never run across another elemental. The lure doesn't work at all on us, doubly so on an earth elemental like me. He kept trying to increase the draw until I had enough and reached out on the elemental plane.

The draw suddenly stopped as I blocked his connection.

He stared at me for a second in shock, then anger washed his face and he lunged forward.

I blocked his slash with my left forearm and, flicking my right wrist, I slashed across his side before stepping back.

Blood soaked his side as he staggered back. His hand went to the wound, then he glared at me and charged.

My small blade slashed him again, deeper, as I whirled to the side, allowing him to careen past me. He spun around with a growl, and I moved into a fighting stance. I didn't want to kill him, but he seemed to be too far gone for reason.

He charged me again.

I slipped sideways and grabbed his arm as he went by, twisting it. With a sweep of my foot, I knocked him to the ground and followed him down, landing on his backside. I hurriedly slapped on the cuffs, pulling his other arm down and back to lock them on him. He started bucking and cussing but I ignored that. However, Louis saying my name brought my head up.

My partner and Doyle were standing behind the two physical manifestations of elements. Louis' gun was in his hand. He had probably tried to fire it and found it didn't work with the manifestations around. Doyle was staring at me like I was a specimen in a petri dish. They had both obviously seen what had happen.

I reached out in the elemental plane again.

The ground under Louis' and Doyle's feet turned to mud and they sank ankle deep. Before they could move, it solidified again, immobilizing them. My first is Earth, that's true. But my secondary is water. However, Fire and Air are capricious with me.

Assured those two wouldn't interfere, I turned my attention back to the perp. "What's your name?"

He cussed me and I slapped him across the back of his head, making it hit the ground hard.

"Ian. Ian, all right."

"Well, Ian, you've really stepped in it."

He tried to glare at me.

"By your actions you have shown that your gift has been warped and that you feel no responsibility or compassion." I paused as I reached across the Aether, the elemental plane, for the third time and found his blocked connection. "Halos," I called. "Reditus."

The leaf tornado creature spun faster, then the leaves exploded and fell to the ground. It was gone.

I cut the connection.

Ian screamed and thrashed, then lay sobbing, as he dropped away from the Aether.

My partner called my name, and I shook my head to clear it. I got to my feet and walked over to them.

Doyle met my eyes defiantly and Louis' face was neutral.

I dismissed my element with a simple “Reditus, then released Doyle's and Louis' feet from the ground. Crossing my arms, I braced myself for whatever was coming next.

Louis holstered his gun, then said, “You've been holding out on me. You took him down like a pro.”

Relief hit me, but I held it in as I looked at Doyle. My partner's words told me he didn't care that I was an elemental or that I hid that tidbit from him. I had counted on our friendship to 'soften' him up, but I was leery of the Lycan. We had no history, and the shifters distrusted elementals, though not to the point that vampires did.

“Those that your partner called 'the old guard' would have us believe that all elementals are like that one.” Doyle pointed to Ian who had somehow curled up in a fetal position and was still sobbing. “But my Grandmere told me a story once when I was a pup. In it elementals were the enforcers for humans, dispensing justice to humans and us Others alike. She said her grandmother had told her the tale when she was a pup.”

“Nature is neither good or evil,” I told him. “It is the human factor that tips the scales.”

We heard running and turned toward the sound just as three officers burst through the trees. They stopped and glanced around. Two then went to Ian while the other came up to us.

I recognized him from the station and greeted him. “Officer Nelson.”

"Detective. What happened here? I gather he's the perp."

"He jumped out of a tree and attacked us," Doyle said before I could say anything. "Detective Finn managed to subdue him."

"You need to have them put a psych hold on him," Louis added. "He's loony tunes."

Nelson nodded.

"How'd you find us?" I asked as I watch them pull Ian to his feet. He was docile and still crying but I didn't trust that that would last.

"Heard a scream and grabbed a couple of guys."

"Good on you, Nelson," Louis said. "Take him back and make sure they put that psych hold on him. We'll be along in a moment."

Nelson nodded again, then gestured for the men to escort Ian away. He gave us all another nod before following the others into the trees back toward the crime scene.

We watched them disappear in the wood, then Louis glared at Doyle. "You hurt her, and I will end you."

"Such talk for a cop," Doyle said with a sly smile.

Louis' eyes went cognac and his fangs dropped.

Doyle laughed and barely got his words out. "Easy, vampire I like her too."

There was a strange emphasis on 'like' that I didn't understand, but the words seemed to calm Louis down. His eyes returned to their warm brown and his fangs retracted.

"This is the beginning of a wonderful relationship," Doyle said with gleaming eyes.

About the Author

Tina Riffey always wanted to be a writer. She started with poetry in grade school and moved to stories by high school. Through a series of moves, she lost those earlier stories, but continued to write down story ideas through the years.

This is the first, a prequel, of the Elemental Detective novella series. Elemental magic, shifters, vampires, and immortals, oh my.

Tina lives in Southern Missouri with a bevy of feral cats

www.ingramcontent.com/pod-product-compliance
Lightning Source LLC
LaVergne TN
LVHW010940110826
845149LV00013B/2689

* 9 7 8 1 9 6 0 4 9 9 2 9 5 *